DISNEP
FROZEN II

Adapted by
Nancy Cote

Illustrated by
Olga Mosqueda

Designed by
Tony Fejeran

A GOLDEN BOOK • NEW YORK

rhcbooks.com
ISBN 978-0-7364-4020-2 (trade) – ISBN 978-0-7364-4021-9 (ebook)
Printed in the United States of America
10 9 8 7 6 5 4 3 2 1

In the kingdom of Arendelle, Anna and Elsa loved the *lullaby* their mother sang to them when they were children.

The lullaby was about a **secret river**,
which held all the answers about the past.
It gave the girls a lot to think about and
excited their *imaginations*.

As time went on, Anna and Elsa grew older. Elsa discovered her magical power over **snow and ice**, which became stronger and stronger. One night, a **mysterious voice** called to her. What did it want?

Elsa realized that the
voice wanted her to travel
north. She went to the fjord
and shot out an enormous

icy blast!

It was clear that Elsa's magic
had done something new and
powerful.
But what did it mean?

The trolls rolled up to the cliffs to let
Elsa know that her blast had awakened
the spirits of the
Enchanted Forest.

They warned her that the spirits were *angry*. The forest was also where a nomadic group of people called the *Northuldra* were said to live.

Elsa knew in her heart that she must follow the mysterious voice to the Enchanted Forest.

Anna and her friends Kristoff, Olaf, and Sven went with Elsa. In the forest, they met the *Wind Spirit*, who whooshed around them.

They also met the Northuldra people, who told them **stories** and revealed that they were more **similar** to Elsa, Anna, and their friends than they were **different**.

While Elsa and her friends were getting to know the Northuldra, the mighty *Fire Spirit* appeared and set the Enchanted Forest on fire!

Elsa tried to **stop** the spreading fire with her magic, but it wasn't working.

Kristoff **helped** Anna and the reindeer escape the flames.

Elsa was finally able to calm the Fire Spirit by feeding it **snowflakes**. The Fire Spirit was actually a little salamander.

Elsa heard the voice again, and she noticed that the Fire Spirit could hear it, too.

Elsa couldn't stay any longer. She had to continue her *journey*. Anna and Olaf joined her, while Kristoff and Sven stayed behind with the Northuldra.

Heading north, Anna and Elsa discovered their ***parents' shipwreck***!

Inside the ship, they studied a map and learned that their parents had traveled north to understand why Elsa had magic.

Elsa feared losing Anna, just as she had lost their parents. Elsa decided to make the rest of the journey alone.

With a heavy heart, Elsa formed a boat made of ice that **scooped up** Anna and Olaf and carried **them** **safely** **away**.

Anna and Olaf loudly **protested**, but there was no way they could stop the boat after Anna accidentally steered it toward the sleeping *Earth Giants*. Anna and Olaf kept quiet as they passed them.

More determined than ever, Elsa
reached the next part of her journey:
the *Dark Sea*. Now she needed
to cross it.

The **Water Nokk** reared up from the sea and tried to stop Elsa. After a fierce battle, Elsa and the Water Nokk realized that their powers were equal. A mutual respect formed between them.

Meanwhile, Anna and Olaf's journey continued into a cave, where an *ice sculpture* appeared in front of them. It was a signal from Elsa. The journey had answered some of the queen's questions.

Elsa had **_finally arrived_** in the north!
The voice that had called to her now quieted to a
whisper, and she realized it had been within her all
along. It had guided her to discover her inner peace.
By working together, the sisters were able to
restore peace and harmony to the land at last.